HORRIBLE HARRY IN ROOM 2B

Miss Mackle asked (Harry) to read his story to the class.

Harry said he met a mermaid, ate a sea turtle, and dug up a treasure.

Miss Mackle put Harry's story up on the bulletin board. She said Harry has lots of ideas.

Harry has never eaten a sea turtle.

Harry has never seen a mermaid.

Harry has never been to sea!

And I know Harry can't even spell "sea." He's horrible at spelling too.

Harry is not like any other second grader in our room. I know all about him.

Harry's my best friend.

"Harry is one of those characters who is made up of parts of children whom readers all know. He is the devilish second grader who plays pranks and gets into mischief but can still be a good friend. Told by his best friend Doug, this story should prove to be popular with those just starting chapter books or looking for a new male character, along with Kline's 'Herbie Jones.'"

—*School Library Journal*

"True to Life"   —*Kirkus Review*

PUFFIN BOOKS ABOUT ROOM 2B

HORRIBLE HARRY IN ROOM 2B

BY SUZY KLINE
Pictures by Frank Remkiewicz

Puffin Books

23

PUFFIN BOOKS

Published by the Penguin Group

Penguin Books USA Inc., 375 Hudson Street, New York, New York 10014, U.S.A.

Penguin Books Ltd, 27 Wrights Lane, London W8 5TZ, England

Penguin Books Australia Ltd, Ringwood, Victoria, Australia

Penguin Books Canada Ltd, 10 Alcorn Avenue, Toronto, Ontario, Canada M4V 3B2

Penguin Books (N.Z.) Ltd, 182-190 Wairau Road, Auckland 10, New Zealand

Penguin Books Ltd, Registered Offices: Harmondsworth, Middlesex, England

First published in the United States of America by Viking Penguin,
a division of Penguin Books USA Inc., 1988
Published in Puffin Books, 1990
Reissued 1997

20 19 18 17 16 15 14 13

THE LIBRARY OF CONGRESS HAS CATALOGED THE PREVIOUS PUFFIN BOOKS
EDITION AS FOLLOWS:

Kline, Suzy. Horrible Harry in room 2B / by Suzy Kline;
pictures by Frank Remkiewicz. p. cm.

"First published in the United States by Viking Penguin in 1988"—T.p. verso.

Summary: Doug discovers that though being Harry's best friend in Miss
Mackle's second grade class isn't always easy, as Harry likes to do
horrible things, it is often a lot of fun.

ISBN 0-14-032825-4

[1. Friendship—Fiction. 2. Schools—Fiction] I. Remkiewicz, Frank, ill.
II. Title [PZ7.K679Ho 1990] [Fic]—dc20 89-36021

This edition ISBN 0-14-038552-5

Printed in the United States of America

RL: 2.3

*Dedicated to my favorite
Harry with love:
Harry C. Weaver 1909–1982
My Dad*

Contents

Horrible Harry in Room 2B

Horrible Harry
and Me

Harry sits next to me in Room 2B. He looks like any other second grader except for one thing.

Harry loves to do horrible things.

When I first met Harry out on the playground, he had a shoebox. I asked him, "What's in there?"

"Something. What's your name?"

"Doug," I said.

"Want to see a girl scream, Doug?"

Before I could say anything, Harry took off after Song Lee. When he trapped her by the tree, he opened up his box and dangled a garter snake in her face.

Song Lee screamed!

That's when I first saw Harry do something horrible.

When it rains, we have recess indoors. Sometimes we play a game called "Seven Up." When it's Harry's turn to be up, everyone wonders, *Will Harry tap me on the head?*

Harry presses his knuckles down hard on your skull.

He calls them knuckle noogies.

Nobody should give anybody a knuckle noogie.

But Harry does.

4

Harry loves to do horrible things.

The second week of school, Sidney called Harry a name. It was during science when we were reading about birds.

"Harry's a canary!" Sidney whispered.

And a lot of kids laughed.

"What's so funny?" the teacher asked.

"Nothing, Miss Mackle," Sidney replied.

Harry didn't think it was nothing. Harry planned to get revenge after school. And he did.

At 3:05, Harry jumped Sidney, pinned him to the ground, and said, "Say *I Love Girls* twice."

"Never!" Sidney said, trying to get away.

"Yeah?"

"Yeah."

And that's when Harry started to

tickle Sidney under the armpits until Sidney couldn't stand it any longer. *"I LOVE GIRLS! I LOVE GIRLS!"* Sidney shouted.

Song Lee, Ida, and Mary heard Sidney.

So did a lot of the boys.

Harry got his revenge all right. And it was horrible.

Sidney ran down the street screaming, "I'll get you back someday!"

When Miss Mackle wants the floor cleaned, she asks Harry to sweep. No one sweeps the floor like Harry. He picks up every piece of paper, every pencil stub, and every bit of clay. Once Harry even crawled under my desk to get a broken crayon!

Nobody knows that Harry *keeps* some of that stuff.

But I do. I sit right next to him and watch. Harry is making stub people!

Harry says his stub people are the scariest creatures in the world. He keeps them in a cigar box in his desk. Someday, when he has made twenty-four, Harry says, his stub people will invade our room.

"It won't be long, Doug," he whispered. "Soon, the stub people will bring *doom* to Room 2B."

When it was Song Lee's birthday, her mother brought in two trays of treats for the class. After we sang "Happy Birthday," Song Lee passed out the treats. Miss Mackle noticed there were three fortune cookies and one cupcake left.

Miss Mackle put them on a plate with a card that said WE LOVE MRS. MICHAELSEN.

Then she said, "Who would like to take these treats to our librarian?"

Everyone raised their hand except Song Lee. She's too shy.

We kept raising our hands. Sidney made noises like, "Oooooo . . . Me! Me! Me!"

Miss Mackle picked Harry and me. She knows we're not afraid to go upstairs where the big kids are.

When we were walking up the stairs to the library, Harry asked me if I wanted to split the cupcake.

"That's for the librarian," I said.

"Mrs. Michaelsen just likes yogurt and carrots," Harry replied. "We'll be doing her a favor."

And so we both promised, "Cross my heart, hope to die, stick a needle in my eye," that we would *never* tell on each another.

Then we ate the librarian's cupcake.

Sometimes Harry gets me to do horrible things.

The day before Columbus Day, Harry came to school with a tattoo on his arm. It was a skull and crossbones. Harry said the sea pirate Long John Silver made his tattoo.

I know Harry did it with a Magic Marker. I think he just wanted to show off in front of Song Lee.

When Harry went to his seat, he took

out his writing folder. He wrote two pages about his adventures at sea.

Miss Mackle asked him to read his story to the class.

Harry said he met a mermaid, ate a sea turtle, and dug up a treasure.

Miss Mackle put Harry's story up on the bulletin board. She said Harry has lots of ideas.

Harry has never eaten a sea turtle.

Harry has never seen a mermaid.

Harry has never been to sea!

And I know Harry can't even spell "sea." He's horrible at spelling too.

Harry is not like any other second grader in our room. I know *all* about him.

Harry's my best friend.

Horrible Harry, the Stub People, and Halloween

The day before Halloween, Harry planned his invasion.

"It's time to bring *doom* to our room, Doug," he said.

I knew what he was talking about. It was time for the invasion of his stub people.

"Do you need help?" I asked.

"You can be my assistant."

14

We put the first pair of stub people in Song Lee's desk while she was up at the pencil sharpener. When she returned, she reached in her desk for a piece of paper.

Harry plugged his ears. "I love it when girls scream," he said. "Look out for *doom!*"

I plugged my ears.

Song Lee didn't scream.

She didn't even jump out of her seat.

Harry and I watched Song Lee play with the stub people. She made them dance on the top of her desk!

Harry scowled. "This is an *invasion*," he complained. "My stub people aren't dancers. They are invaders! They bring *doom* to our room!"

I nodded.

Harry leaned over and whispered.

"*Next* time, we have to catch the enemy by *real* surprise."

When Harry and I got permission to go to the bathroom, we stopped in the hallway. We slipped some stub people in Sidney's sweater sleeves.

Perfect, we thought.

When it came time to line up for lunch, Harry and I waited.

Slowly, Sidney put on his sweater.

And we watched.

Sidney would jump up and scream any minute now!

But when Sidney put his arm in the sleeve, the stub people fell through and landed on the floor.

Sidney never saw them.

Neither did Ida or Mary. They stepped on them!

Harry kneeled down and scraped the stub people off the floor. Gently, he wrapped them in his handkerchief.

We buried them in the garbage during lunch recess. And we gave them a farewell salute.

"This means war!" Harry exclaimed. "We've lost too many men. We have to invade the mainland now."

"What's the mainland?" I asked.

"You'll see," Harry said.

Just before the bell rang, Harry put

two pairs of stub people on the teacher's desk.

"The *teacher's desk?*" I said.

"The teacher's desk," Harry repeated. "Prepare for *doom* in our room!"

Then he sat up straight and folded his hands on his desk.

When the bell rang, Miss Mackle walked in. "I can see Harry is ready for class," she said.

"Plug your ears," Harry whispered as Miss Mackle walked to her desk. "She's going to scream and jump right out the window."

"What's this?" Miss Mackle said when she saw the stub people.

Harry took his fingers out of his ears.

I did too.

"How cute!" Miss Mackle exclaimed as she held one up.

"Cute?" Harry said.

"Cute?" I said. Harry and I gave each other a look. How could that be? The stub people are the scariest creatures on earth.

Harry put his head down on his desk, and buried his face in his arms.

Sometimes it's real hard for Harry to be horrible.

"Cheer up," I said, "tomorrow's Halloween. That's your favorite holiday. You'll be real scary then."

Harry looked up. "Halloween . . . " He grinned.

Nobody knew what Harry was going to be for Halloween, but everybody knew it would be something horrible.

Just before the 3 o'clock bell rang, we talked about it.

"Are you going to be Frankenstein?" Ida asked Harry.

Harry flashed his white teeth. "Scarier than that."

"Are you going to be a skeleton?" Mary said.

Harry shook his head. "Much, much scarier than that."

"Are you going to be a vampire?" Song Lee asked.

Harry shook his head again, "You'll never guess."

Sidney said, "Oh yes, I will. I bet you're going to be a canary!" And he laughed and laughed.

"Just beware, Sidney. Halloween is tomorrow." Then Harry leaned forward and shouted, "BOO!"

Sidney jumped a foot in the air.

The next morning in school, everyone watched the door and waited for Harry.

When a huge witch came in, everyone shivered. "It's *Harry!*" they shouted.

And then the witch took off her green mask. "Good morning, boys and girls," a voice said.

It was Miss Mackle!

After we said the pledge, I looked over at Harry's seat. It was empty. Where was Harry?

And then, at 9:05, a very big Count Dracula showed up at the door.

Everyone really shivered!

"It's *Harry!*" they shouted.

And then a voice said, "Happy Halloween, boys and girls."

It was the principal, Mr. Cardini.

Then, at 9:10, something slithered into the room. It was long and striped. It had a thin red tongue.

"Aaaauuugh!" screamed Sidney.

Miss Mackle walked over to look. "And who are you?" she asked.

The snake slithered across the classroom floor, and everyone screamed!

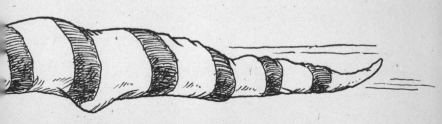

The snake went "Sssssss . . ."

Miss Mackle started to tap her foot. "If it's who I think it is, you're ten minutes late for school."

Everyone leaned forward to see.

A head popped out of the snake skin, and flashed his white teeth.

"Harry!" everyone shouted.

"You're late," Miss Mackle said.

"Snakes don't move that quickly," Harry replied. "It took me a long time to slither across the playground."

"Well, you'll have to make up the extra time after school," Miss Mackle said. "Ten minutes."

Harry made a face.

Sidney beamed. "My watch says nine-twelve."

Harry glared at Sidney.

Sometimes Harry is so horrible he has to stay after school.

Harry's Triple Revenge

Sidney brought a book of bird stickers to Room 2B. He said he had a page of blue jays, a page of robins, and a page of something else.

"What's the something else?" Ida asked.

"It's a secret," Sidney said, looking at Harry.

Harry lowered his eyebrows. "I know

what the other stickers are. Don't you, Doug?"

I did when I looked at Harry's chair.

There was a yellow canary sticker stuck to it.

Sidney laughed. "Harry's a canary."

Ida and Song Lee tried not to laugh.

Harry held up his fist. I knew what he was thinking. *Revenge!*

At noon, we lined up to go to the cafeteria. Harry got his lunch box down from the shelf. Then he noticed something.

A yellow canary sticker was stuck to his lunch box.

This time Harry held up two fists.

I knew what that meant.

Double revenge!

When we got to the cafeteria table, Harry didn't say anything. He just bit into a banana and stared at Sidney.

After lunch our class walked upstairs to the library. Harry went right to the section with books about snakes, slugs, and sea turtles.

Mrs. Michaelsen tapped Harry on the shoulder. "I have a new book for you, Harry."

Harry turned. "You do?"

"Just came in today." And then she whispered, "It's horrible."

Harry flashed his white teeth as he looked at the title of the book: *Terrible Tyrannosaurus Rex*.

"Thanks, Mrs. Michaelsen. You're the best librarian in the world."

Mrs. Michaelsen patted Harry on the head, and then she helped me find a good book on Indians.

Harry and I sat down at the reading table and read our books. We didn't think of a canary once.

When we went back to Room 2B, Harry put his dinosaur book under his lunch box because he wanted to take it home.

At 3 P.M., when the bell rang, we got our jackets, lunch boxes, and books.

That was when Harry saw it . . .

A yellow canary sticker stuck to *Terrible Tyrannosaurus Rex*!

Harry was so mad his eyebrows came together.

Harry gritted his teeth and carefully pulled the canary sticker off the plastic book cover. *"This means triple revenge!"* he growled.

At 3:05, Harry spotted Sidney by the big bush. "Wait up!" he called. "I want to tell you something."

Sidney waited.

"I just wanted to shake your hand," Harry said.

Sidney scratched his head. "You do?"

"Sure, that was a real neat trick you did today. You put a yellow canary sticker on my chair, my lunch box, and then on my new library book. You're one funny guy."

"Well," Sidney replied, "nothing like a good laugh."

"Yeah," Harry said. "So, I just wanted to shake your hand and let you know how I feel about things."

Sidney put out his hand.

Harry shook it.

"Hey!" Sidney said, jerking his hand away and looking at it. "What's this yellow and brown slime in my hand?"

Harry made his teeth show as he smiled. "It *was* a slug."

"*Aaaauuuugh!*" Sidney screamed. "I squeezed a slimy slug! Help!" He ran down the sidewalk shaking his hand in the air.

Harry closed his lunch box. "Well, Doug, a leftover banana packs a lot of power."

"Especially for triple revenge," I said.

Harry wiped his hands on his jeans. "The guy had it coming. You don't fool around with *Terrible Tyrannosaurus Rex,*" he said as he tucked the book under his arm. "Or . . . *me.*"

I nodded.

Because it was the horrible truth.

Horrible Harry
and the
Thanksgiving Play

Miss Mackle said that Room 2B was putting on a Thanksgiving play for the parents.

"Some of you will be Pilgrims, some of you will be Indians, and one of you will be Squanto."

"I want to be Squanto," I said. "I want

to show the Pilgrims how to plant corn with dead fish bodies."

Miss Mackle looked out the window.

When she looked back, she said, "Okay, Doug, you can be Squanto."

"I want to be the dead fish body," Harry said.

Miss Mackle stared at Harry. "You want to be a dead fish in our Thanksgiving play?"

Everyone in the class looked at Harry.

Harry beamed. "It's an important role. If it wasn't for the dead fish, the Pilgrims wouldn't have been able to fertilize the corn and if the corn wasn't fertilized, the corn wouldn't have grown and the Pilgrims would have starved and you wouldn't have a play about them. So, I want to be a dead fish."

"But that's a horrible part to play . . .

a dead fish!" Miss Mackle said, making a face.

Harry flashed his white teeth. "I don't mind."

Of course Harry wouldn't mind. Harry loves to do horrible things.

At the first practice, Song Lee got sick.

All she had to say was "Life is hard." She was a Pilgrim. But she just mumbled.

"You have to speak up," Miss Mackle said.

Song Lee looked like she was going to cry.

"Do you not feel well?" Miss Mackle asked.

Song Lee shook her head.

Ten minutes later, Song Lee went home.

Everyone knew why. Song Lee wasn't

really sick. She was just too scared to say anything in front of anybody.

"Okay, places, everybody," Miss Mackle called. "Pilgrims, you are in the field sowing. Squanto, you come in and say your line about helping them plant corn. Pilgrims, you talk among yourselves about how hard life is."

Everyone did what Miss Mackle said except Harry.

"You wiggle forward when Squanto pulls you on the rope," Miss Mackle said.

"I don't feel like wiggling right now," Harry said.

"But you have to wiggle a little so that Squanto can pull you in," Miss Mackle replied. "You're too heavy."

"I'll wiggle a little," Harry grumbled.

I could tell Harry wasn't his old self. He didn't feel like being a dead fish.

After school Harry came to my house.

He called Song Lee on my phone. And then he talked with her mother.

I wondered if Harry's bad mood had something to do with Song Lee's going home.

The next day at practice, Song Lee showed up. She whispered something in Miss Mackle's ear. Miss Mackle leaned back against the chalkboard. She looked shocked. Finally she smiled.

"Okay, places, everybody," she called. "Pilgrims, you are in the field sowing. Squanto, you come in with your two fish."

"Two?" I said.

"Two?" the class said.

Miss Mackle cleared her throat. "Song Lee would like to be a dead fish also."

The class looked down at Song Lee and Harry.

Science Fair
Tuesday
Egg Drop 1:00 PM
Balloon Busting
Device 2:00 PM
Exhibits - All day

I looked down.

They were lying on the floor. Dead. Saying nothing.

"And Song Lee's mother made fish tails and fish fins for them. Isn't that wonderful?"

I could tell Harry thought it was wonderful. He was playing a dead fish that smiled.

"Places, everyone," Miss Mackle called again.

Everyone did what Miss Mackle said. I said my line real well. And when I got

to the part about fertilizing the corn with dead fish, I had a rope around Harry's waist and Song Lee's waist to slide them in.

They both wiggled forward.

So it was easy.

Sometimes Harry's horrible ideas help the class.

Horrible Harry
and the
Field Trip

Harry and I made a promise. We said, "Cross my heart, hope to die, stick a needle in my eye," that we were going to be partners for our field trip.

Three *weeks* ago!

The morning of the field trip, *just* when the bus pulled up in front of South School, Harry said, "Doug, I can't be your partner."

"Why?" I asked.

"Song Lee doesn't have a partner. Her partner is home with the flu."

"Great!" I said. "So now *I* get to be the one with no partner."

"You can tough it out," Harry said. Then he flashed his ugly white teeth and sat down next to Song Lee on the bus.

Harry *really* is horrible!

I sat in front of him next to Miss Mackle.

"Do you want the window seat?" she asked.

I shook my head. I wanted to sit on the aisle, across from Sidney.

Sidney leaned over and said, "Forget Harry. He's a canary."

Harry looked over and held up a fist.

I made a face. "Harry *is* a canary. *Tweet! Tweet! Tweet!*"

Now Harry had *both* fists in the air.

That's when I sat back and talked with Miss Mackle. "What do you have in your lunch?" I asked her.

"Cream cheese on date-nut bread, celery, and dried apricots."

It sounded like something my teacher would eat.

"What do you have in your lunch, Doug?"

"Jelly sandwich, apple, and six giant *chocolate chip cookies*." I said the last part real loud.

Harry leaned over the bus seat and drooled.

"Mom packed me *extras* for my partner," I said.

Harry licked his lips.

"Do you like chocolate chip cookies?" I asked Miss Mackle.

"I love them," she said.

"I do too," Harry said.

"Sit down, Harry," Miss Mackle scolded.

Harry made a face.

I noticed Song Lee was talking to Mary and Ida across the aisle.

Harry just kept staring out the window. He had no one to talk to.

When we got to the aquarium, Miss

Mackle and I were line leaders. We led the class into the building and into the room with the big tropical-fish tanks.

Just when I was looking at the upside-down catfish, Harry said, "Do you want to be partners?"

I gave him a look. "I wouldn't be your partner in a thousand years."

"I'll wait," Harry said.

When I was through looking at the upside-down catfish, I said, "I thought you were partners with Song Lee."

"She's with her two other friends, Mary and Ida. They're going to sit three on a seat on the way home."

"I wouldn't be your partner in a hundred years," I said.

"I'll wait," Harry replied.

At lunch everyone sat at picnic tables. I sat next to Sidney.

That was when a bee landed on my jelly sandwich.

I didn't move.

Sidney screamed.

Harry grabbed his paper cup and trapped the bee on my bread. Then he took the sandwich with the cup on top of it and walked it to the trash can.

Harry dropped the bee inside the can and closed the flap. "Some jerk is gonna get a *big* surprise when he opens this!" he said.

Then Harry offered me half of his sardine sandwich.

"No thanks," I said. "I can't eat sardines now. They look too much like the fish in the aquarium."

Harry stared at his sardine sandwich. He looked sick.

He ran to the trash can and threw it in.

That was when Harry got *his* big surprise.

The bee flew out of the trash can and stung Harry on the cheek!

Boy, did Harry yell!

I felt bad for him.

Miss Mackle got out her first-aid kit and put something on Harry's bee sting.

When it was time to go, Harry got on the bus first and sat in the back seat by the window.

Alone.

As I walked up the bus aisle, Sidney moved over. "Want to share a seat with us, Doug? You don't want to sit with that canary Harry."

That's when I made a fist. "Don't call Harry a canary."

And I went over and sat down next to Harry.

"You don't think I'm a jerk?" he asked.

I shook my head. He did try to help me. He got stung because of me. I reached into my lunch bag and handed Harry my last chocolate chip cookie.

"Thanks, pal," he said, and he ate every crumb.

Harry isn't always horrible.

Just once in a while.

About the Author

SUZY KLINE graduated from the University of California at Berkeley and received her elementary school teacher's credential from California State University at Hayward. She has been an elementary school teacher for many years and lives in Torrington, Connecticut with her husband and two daughters.

About the Illustrator

FRANK REMKIEWICZ is a graduate of the Arts Center School in Los Angeles. In addition to having illustrated over twenty books for children, Remkiewicz also provided the illustrations for the box of an ever-popular brand of animal crackers. He is married, has three children, and lives in Guerneville, California.

4/05

FICTION

BAKER & TAYLOR